The Great Cl

Fore

CW00854273

These stories are dedicated to my late friend, Nick Hayes.

He was a wonderful singer, musical arranger and teacher; a great inspiration to all who met him.

Nick got me involved in singing with the Rolling Hills Chorus; something I enjoyed for many years.

The RHC goes from strength to strength today and I wish them well in their own 'Great Chorus Contests'.

I'm not sure which of the choruses in this book the RHC resembles the most but its members certainly have as much fun as any of these made-up characters.

I'd also like to thank Angus Jamieson (bass) and Andrew Watt (baritone). Together with Nick (tenor) we had fun as the Moonglow Barbershop Quartet.

GJ Abercrombie

Edinburgh

2021

The Dancing Rabbit Chorus

(Can they win the contest?)

For Nick

and the Rolling Hills Chorus

Chapter 1

Tali Has an Idea

Tali Bookhound was driving through Musselburgh in Esmerelda, his library-van. He saw his friend Mrs O'Hare walking along the pavement with a large folder under her arm. He tooted Esmerelda's horn and waved to her as he parked the van beside a large grassy area called 'the Links'.

Mrs O'Hare waved back and walked over to meet Tali as he opened Esmerelda's door.

"Hello, Tali," she said. "It's nice to see you again."

"It's lovely to see you too, Mrs O'Hare," replied Tali.

Mrs O'Hare looked in Esmeralda's door and got a nice surprise.

"I see you still have the guitar magnet I bought for you in Memphis when we went on our magical musical tour of America," she said.

The magnet was stuck to the side of Tali's desk in the van beside lots of others he had been given by people whom he and Esmerelda had helped.

(Can you see the magnet that is shaped like a guitar?)

"Oh, yes," said Tali. "That was a great trip. But what brings you to Musselburgh? I thought you lived in Portobello, beside Trevor."

"That's right," she replied. "I do live in Portobello and Trevor still lives in the flat next door. Our friend Declan has moved from Leith to Musselburgh. He now has a bigger house with stairs inside! We use his new place to practise our singing and dancing because there is so much space."

"Is it not quite far for everyone to travel?" asked Tali.

"Oh no," she replied. "Trevor cycles his bike and I can get the number 26 bus. It only takes ten minutes from Portobello. Some of the other rabbits take the train from Edinburgh and that's even quicker."

"I'm on my way to a chorus rehearsal at Declan's house now, if you'd like to come along," she added.

Tali was delighted to be invited to a rehearsal of the famous *Dancing Rabbit Chorus*.

Mrs O'Hare was the chorus leader (or Musical Director as she liked to be called) and the large folder under her arm contained the music for the songs she was going to teach the singers that day.

When they arrived at Declan's house, many rabbits were already there, chatting noisily to each other.

Declan had kindly made them a pot of tea and some yummy fairy cakes.

Tali already knew many of the rabbits because they had appeared in the play he had directed recently. The play was about a dragon who lived in a windmill and it was very successful. It was also very funny; especially when the fox threw <u>flour</u> onto the stage at the end instead of <u>flowers</u>.

(Do you remember that?)

Tali said, "Hello" to everyone and was introduced to some new rabbits by his friend Trevor (the Rabbit with Three Ears). Trevor and Declan (the Rabbit with Ten Ears!) were great pals and had enjoyed many adventures together.

The rabbits were having fun remembering the time when lots of them had pretended to be Trevor by each borrowing one of Declan's ten ears. They had done this to confuse the naughty fox who was disguised as a policeman. Mr Fox had said he wanted to take Trevor to jail but the rabbits had 'out-foxed' him by making up lots of 'rabbits with three ears'.

(Do you remember that too?)

Soon it was time for the rehearsal to start and Mrs O'Hare tapped her baton on her music-stand to stop all the chatting.

When they were all quiet, she said: "I'm pleased to welcome Mr Tali Bookhound to our rehearsal. Many of you will know him from the stage play which he arranged and directed recently. I hope you will all sing and dance really well today to show him what we can do."

Tali sat on a chair and watched and listened to them performing their favourite songs.

During one song, Mrs O'Hare stopped the singing and asked why there was a big space at Trevor's left-hand-side.

"No-one wants to stand there because his smelly, left foot is really stinky tonight," said one of the rabbits. "Everyone wants to be on the other side, next to his lovely-smelling right foot."

Some rabbits even tried putting pegs on their noses to avoid the smell but then they could not sing properly. The notes came out all wobbly.

(Have you tried singing while holding your nose?)

Declan went and fetched the basin from his kitchen and filled it with soapy, lemony water. He told Trevor to stand with his left foot in it while they were singing.

This worked a treat and the smell disappeared … but it meant that water splashed everywhere when Trevor danced!

At the end of the rehearsal, Tali asked Mrs O'Hare if her chorus had ever considered entering a competition. She said that she had never thought about that and wondered if they would be good enough.

Tali said that he thought they were fantastic … and then he had an idea!

He said he would be happy to arrange a singing competition.

Mrs O'Hare thought about it for a moment. The rabbits were all staring at her, hoping she would agree to do it. Some were nodding enthusiastically.

Finally, she said that she thought the rabbits would be delighted to enter.

"We all love singing so much!" she said.

"And dancing!" shouted Trevor. "We love dancing too!"

Tali laughed and said, "I'll contact all the friends who took part in our play and see if any of them would like to enter a choir for the competition."

Tali decided to call it …

'The Great Chorus Contest'

Chapter 2

Advertising the Contest

Mrs O'Hare had already agreed that her chorus would enter the contest so Tali knew that there would be at least one entry; but he wondered how he could let others know about the competition.

He sat at his desk inside the library-van thinking about various options:

- Printing fliers; like he did for his Drama Club
  - This uses a lot of paper and some people just throw them in the bin.
- Television
  - Most people just fast-forward through adverts when watching their programmes on TV.
- Radio
  - There are too many different radio stations and it would be expensive to advertise on all of them.
- Newspapers
  - No-one really reads newspapers anymore. They get their news on their mobile phones.

Suddenly, Esmerelda's door flew open … all by itself.

"That's strange," thought Tali as he stood up and closed it.

Then it flew open again!

Tali went over to pull the door shut once more but it would not move; it was stuck!

He ran outside to try closing the door from there and suddenly it slammed shut on its own.

"That's VERY strange," he thought.

Tali tried to open the door again but found that it was locked. He was pulling hard on the door handle when, suddenly, he noticed a big brown box stuck to Esmeralda's side.

"Eh? That was not there earlier," Tali thought to himself.

Clever Esmerelda had magicked-up a letter-box under the window on her door.

The box had a large slot at the top and writing which said:

"Great Chorus Contest … Post Your Entry Form Here".

Tali dashed into the van through the door which Esmerelda had now unlocked.

He sat at his desk to make a large, colourful poster.

Tali then stuck the poster to the side of Esmerelda right next to her letter-box. He was sure that everyone would see it as he travelled around the country lending out books and helping people.

Tali added 'Venue to be decided' because he thought he would have to wait and see how many choruses would enter the competition, how many singers would be in each chorus and where they all lived.

He could then choose a venue which was big enough for all the singers and which was near where most of them lived.

In a bag, beside the post-box, Tali left a bundle of entry forms which the choruses had to fill in, giving details of:

- Chorus Name
- Musical Director
- Number of Members
- Dancing included? (YES/NO)
- Where they live

The entry form also told them that they should prepare two songs: one fast song and one slow song.

The songs they chose should be kept secret from the other choruses so that they would be a surprise on the day of the contest.

When the forms were completed, they were to be posted through the slot in the letter-box.

All week, Tali was very excited and wanted to know if anyone had entered the competition but he was very good and was determined not to peek until after the closing date for entries.

"I'll look in the box on Saturday morning," he said to himself. "I hope there are lots of entries. What good is a competition with only one team?"

Chapter 3

The Contest Entrants

On Friday night, as Tali went up to his bed in the roof of the library-van he thought he would never sleep; he was too excited, wondering how many groups had entered the contest.

Esmerelda was looking forward to the morning too because she already knew how many entries there were in the box. After all, it was her box, attached to her door.

Tali squeezed his eyes tightly shut and tried his best to fall asleep.

Esmerelda played him some soothing lullaby music on the van's radio and opened the bedroom curtains so that Tali could see the stars. This usually helped him to fall asleep.

Tali finally fell into a deep, deep sleep. He snored very loudly.

ZZZZZZZZZZZZZ

On Saturday morning, Tali was still sleeping at 9 o'clock. This surprised Esmerelda as she thought he'd be up early to look in the box.

She played some loud music through her radio but Tali just turned over and hugged his pillow tightly.

She then played a recording of some local children shouting, "Wake Up, Tali!" at the top of their voices.

This did the trick!

Tali's eyes sprang open and he sat up in bed so quickly that he bumped his head on the roof.

"What.. what.. what's going on?" said Tali, rubbing his eyes. Then he remembered what day it was.

It was … SATURDAY … TIME TO OPEN THE BOX!

He quickly dreeped down from his bed in the roof of the library-van.

He opened the door in his pyjamas *(funny place to put a door)* and stepped outside.

When he peered into the letter-box, Tali got a surprise … it was empty!

"Oh no!" he sighed. "No-one wants to enter my contest! Not even *the Dancing Rabbit Chorus*. But, Mrs O'Hare promised me that they would enter."

Sadly and slowly, he climbed back into the library-van. He was about to make his breakfast when he heard the magic books on the shelves whispering to one another.

They were nudging each other and saying, "You tell him … No, you tell him … No, <u>you</u> tell him." Finally, a little book with the title *'That's Not My Sausage'* flew out from its place on the shelf and whispered in Tali's ear:

"Have a look on your desk, Mr Bookhound."

When Tali turned around and looked, he saw a neat pile of entry forms lying there in the middle of his desk. Clever Esmerelda had already emptied her letter-box for him as a surprise!

Tali sat at his desk and started to look at the entry forms. Here's what he saw:

The Dancing Rabbit Chorus

- Musical Director: Mrs I L O'Hare
- Members: 12
- From: Musselburgh, Scotland
- Dancing?: Of course, it's in our name!

Tali thought, "Well I knew that *the Dancing Rabbit Chorus* were going to enter the contest and it's good that they have 12 members."

He then wondered what the initials 'I' and 'L' stood for in Mrs O'Hare's name. He decided he would ask her the next time they met.

(What do you think her first names might be?)

The Magical Musicians

- Musical Director: Mary Mouse
- Members: 6
- From: Camberwell, London
- Dancing?: Yes (and gymnastics)

(Do you remember Mary and Martha?)

(Martha the Magical Mouse is Trevor's cousin. She and her musical friend, Mary, have had lots of adventures with Trevor and Declan.)

Tali remembered that Mary and Martha had helped with his play. Mary had arranged the music and Martha (who is secretly magical) had done all the sound effects and lighting.

Their group was quite small but he was sure that they would be good with Mary in charge. She is very musical and can play tunes on anything: pots and pans, tins of beans, cardboard boxes ... anything.

The Dawn Chorus

- Musical Director: Bertie Blackbird
- Members: About 100
- From: The Visitor Nest, Princes Street Gardens, Edinburgh
- Dancing?: Yes, if you include murmuration

Tali thought this was a good name for a chorus. Dawn is when the sun starts to shine in the morning and he often hears birds singing then.

He was a bit concerned that they had 100 members but thought it might be fine if they were all small birds like blackbirds and robins. If they were turkeys or ostriches, he'd have to find a huge venue for the competition.

Murmuration is where birds make moving shapes in the sky as they fly in formation. Again, Tali hoped it would only be small birds doing this!

The Supercat Chorus

- Musical Director: Gerard Supercat
- Members: 10
- From: Corstorphine, Edinburgh, Scotland
- Dancing?: Flying only

Gerard had recently been promoted to be a proper Supercat and had his own flying cape. He no longer needed his scooter to keep up with Misha.

Tali remembered that Gerard could sometimes be a bit clumsy, even with his Supercat cape.

(Do you remember when he mixed up the plans of a boat he was building and made a rocket instead?)

He did make a good job selling tickets for the play so maybe he'd do well as a chorus director.

The Rappers

- Musical Director: Mr N Fox
- Members: 7
- From: Musselburgh, Scotland
- Dancing?: No, No, No

Tali knew that rapping was a type of modern music and so was looking forward to hearing them. He was a bit worried that their musical director was a Mr N Fox. He hoped it was not the Mr Naughty Fox who had stolen Trevor's shoes and some of Tali's own books from Esmerelda.

(Do you remember these stories?)

He was extra worried when he saw that this chorus came from Musselburgh, which is where this trouble-maker lives.

If it really was this same tricky fox, Tali wondered who the other six members of his chorus might be.

"I hope it's not the birds who tried to cheat at the Avian Games," he thought to himself.

(We'll soon find out!)

In total, there were five choruses entering the contest.

Tali was quite pleased with this number.

He thought about each of them in turn and decided he would visit them all during their rehearsals to explain the rules of the competition and to agree upon a suitable venue.

Tali imagined the trouble there would be if the fox and the raptors were together in the same chorus.

Chapter 4

The Magical Musicians

Tali's first visit was to *the Magical Musicians* who were based in Camberwell in South London.

He thought their chorus name was an interesting choice. He knew that Mary Mouse was very musical because she arranged all the music for his play. He suspected that Martha might be a bit magical but he could not be sure. She had somehow managed to produce lots of sound effects for the show even when she did not seem to have any equipment.

Very strange!

He was used to magical things anyway because he lived in Esmerelda, a magical library-van filled with magical books.

He could have driven the library-van all the way to London to visit the 'Magical Musicians' but that would have taken a whole day. Instead, Tali took a book about London from the travel section of the library and placed it on the book-stand on his desk.

As soon as Tali opened the magic book, Esmerelda closed her door and the other books started to spin around like a whirlpool.

Tali and Esmerelda were on their way to London!

When the books stopped spinning and Esmerelda opened her door, Tali saw that they were parked in Camberwell Green, a large, grassy area surrounded by busy roads and lots of shops.

He knew that they were close to where Mary and Martha lived because he remembered that this was where Trevor had parked his helicopter when he and Declan came to London for the Queen's Royal Garden Party.

Tali realised that he did not know exactly where the mice practised their singing. He listened carefully and thought he could hear music. He saw a wooden spoon being waved about in the air through the window of Camberwell Library.

He thought there must be a baking lesson going on in there.

Tali went over to have a closer look in the library window.

When he peeked through the window of the library, he got a nice surprise. He could see Mary Mouse conducting her singers using a wooden spoon from her kitchen as a baton.

Tali went into the library and stood at the back of the room until they had finished their song. It was 'My Own Home' from the Jungle Book film and they sang it really well.

"That was great," said Tali. "You should sing that in the contest."

"Maybe we will," replied Mary, thoughtfully. "It's nice to see you, Tali. We were just about to have a break for a cup of tea. Why don't you join us and tell us all about it."

Tali sat at a table with all the mice from the chorus. Besides Mary and Martha there were three others: Monica, Morris and Melissa.

(Do you remember them from the fashion show which Martha and Mary put on in this very library a while ago?)

"I see there are only five of you today. Your entrance form says that there are six in the chorus," said Tali.

"Oh, yes. Peter can't make it today because he had to stay in late after school. He's been naughty," said Martha.

"As usual," said Mary, huffily.

(Do you remember what name Mary calls him? ...)

(... 'Peter, the cheater' or 'Pete, the cheat' for short)

"Peter may join us later," added Martha.

"Now," said Tali. "I have a favour to ask you. There are four choruses from Scotland and only one from England. I wonder if you would mind terribly if we hold the contest near Edinburgh. Since yours is the smallest chorus, it would also mean the fewest competitors having to travel."

"That's not a problem," said Martha, smiling knowingly at Mary. "We can use the Library Link to get there."

"Oh? What's that?" asked Tali.

Martha was a bit shy to say anything so Mary blurted it out.

"It's a special way that Martha has for getting from one library to another. She uses it to visit her Granny Lucy in Corstorphine Library."

"Oh that's great then," said Tali, winking at Martha. "I'll let you know which library is nearest to the venue when I've spoken to all the other choruses."

"That's great!" squeaked Mary Mouse with excitement. "I love Edinburgh!"

Just then, they all heard a lot of shouting coming from outside the library. It was accompanied by Esmerelda's horn tooting loudly.

When they ran out to the street, they saw Pete the Cheat sitting in the driving-seat of the library-van.

He was soaking wet and could not get out because Esmerelda had locked him inside.

Tali opened the driver's door and Pete fell out onto the pavement into a big, deep puddle.

He could not get any wetter than he already was.

"What's going on?" asked Tali.

"I just wanted a shot of pretend-driving so I opened the door and jumped in," screeched Peter. "I pulled the lever for the wipers to skoosh water on the windows but the water came up the <u>inside</u> of the glass instead of the <u>outside</u>."

All the other mice giggled and pointed at Pete who was dripping water all over the place.

"Well, you'll know better next time. Do <u>not</u> mess about with Esmerelda!" said Tali.

Esmerelda showed off by squirting water up the <u>outside</u> of her windscreen and then drying it with her wipers.

Mary handed a towel to Peter and said, "Right everyone! Let's get back inside and sing. We still have a lot of practising to do."

Tali turned to Mary and Martha and said:

"I think it's time for me to go home now. Good luck with your rehearsals. See you in Scotland for the competition!"

Chapter 5

The Rappers

When Tali arrived in Musselburgh for the rehearsal of the chorus called *'The Rappers'*, he was concerned to see that it was indeed the Mr N Fox who had stolen from Esmerelda. Tali remembered the house from the last time when he had come to rescue his books.

It still had the same green door and the same old purple/blue curtains in the sitting-room downstairs.   Tali rang the doorbell and waited patiently.

As he stood outside on the pavement, he could hear a terrible noise coming from inside. It was loud screeching and squawking like someone had dropped a fridge on an elephant's foot.

"These guys are not likely to win a singing competition if they keep fighting among themselves," thought Tali to himself.

He was finally invited into the living-room by the sly fox.

"Ah, come in Tali. You are most welcome," said the Fox. "Look guys, it's Tali Bookhound," he told his friends.

Tali soon discovered that the other members of the chorus were all large birds; just as he had feared; vultures, ospreys and hawks, all fighting. There were feathers flying everywhere!

What a mess!

"Hello Molly," said one of the hawks, with a grin.

"Actually, my name is Tali, thanks."

"Whatever!" said the cheeky hawk. "We used to call ourselves *'The Raptors'* when we competed in the Avian Games but we have decided that *'The Rappers'* is a more suitable name to use for this contest."

"Very clever," said Tali, not really thinking it was clever at all. He had heard all about their antics at the games. "I've come here to tell you about the rules of the competition."

"We'd rather hear about the prize, Collie," said a vulture.

"You have to sing two songs …."

"Tell us about the prize, Polly," said a greedy osprey, interrupting Tali.

" … one slow song and one fast song," Tali continued, ignoring the interruption.

"Tell us about the prize, Holly," said a hawk.

"The details of the prize are on the poster which you have all seen so you should know what it is," snapped Tali, getting angry. "You can sing any songs you like but it would be best if you did not tell anyone else which songs you have chosen. Other choruses will not tell you which songs they are performing either. That way it will be a nice surprise for everyone on the day of the contest."

Tali could see that they were not really listening to him. All they were interested in was the prize … and calling him silly names.

Mr Fox pretended to be nice. He said to the birds, "Don't be rude to Mr Bookhound. Remember he is one of the judges of the competition."

"Who cares?" they replied.

After Tali had left, a vulture said, "Stupid contest. Who wants to sing anyway?"

"But the prize is £50!" said the two ospreys together. "Think what we could buy with that money."

The six birds argued amongst themselves about what they would spend the money on.

Mr Fox said that he wished they could find out which songs the other entrants were going to sing.

"We could then learn those songs and sing along badly with them. That would ruin them and we would win. Yes, we must find out their songs!"

While the birds shouted at each other, Mr Fox was hatching a plan about how to discover what the other choruses' songs were.

(He's always hatching plans, isn't he? I wonder what this one will be!)

Chapter 6

The Dancing Rabbit Chorus

Since Tali was already in Musselburgh, he decided to visit *the Dancing Rabbit Chorus* next.

When he arrived at Declan's house, the postman was struggling with a huge parcel.

"Let me help you with that," said Tali and he took one end of the box.

It was really heavy!

When they got inside, some of the rabbits were there but Declan was missing.

"We'll just leave the parcel in the corner of the room," said Tali to the postman.

"Where's Declan got to?" he asked the assembled singers.

"He's gone to the shop to buy some chocolate biscuits for our break," said Mrs O'Hare. "I think we should start the rehearsal with a few of our favourite songs. We'll not practise our competition songs until everyone is here."

This was a very lucky decision by Mrs O'Hare because there was something that she did not know. The naughty fox was hiding inside the large box, spying on them; he had posted himself to Declan's house!

He had cut small holes in the box so that he could breathe and also so that he could listen to their rehearsal in secret.

He listened to their warm-up songs and giggled to himself:

"This is a great plan. I'll hear which songs they are going to sing and then I can report back to the *Rappers*. We'll soon spoil their performance."

Since Trevor has three ears he has great hearing and could hear someone giggling somewhere. He did not realise it was the fox in the box but he knew something was not quite right.

When Declan returned from the shop, he saw the large box in the corner and wondered what it could be.

"I'll open it after our competition songs," he said. Mr Fox was very excited at this and giggled a bit more. Trevor was even more suspicious of the strange parcel.

"Why don't you open it now?" he asked Declan. "I'm sure we'd all love to know what's inside."

"Oh-oh," thought the fox. "What will I do?"

"Do you mind, Mrs O'Hare? I'm happy to leave it until later," said Declan.

"PHEW!" The fox heaved a sigh of relief!

"It's OK, Declan. Please do open your parcel now. I wonder what it is too," said Mrs O'Hare.

"Oh No!" thought the fox.

As Declan started to cut the string on the parcel, the fox had an idea. He would pretend to be a statue. He put out his paws as if he were playing a piano and froze solid.

When the box was opened, everyone gasped!

"A statue of that ugly fox," said one of the rabbits. "Who would send you that?"

Mr Fox was annoyed at being called 'ugly' but managed not to show it.

He stood very still with a fixed smile on his face.

After a while, one of the rabbits put a lamp-shade over the fox's head and said, "There, we don't have to look at his stupid grin anymore."

Mr Fox was not pleased at being made into a lamp. He could no longer see what was going on in the room but at least he could still hear.

"Right!" said Mrs O'Hare. "Get your contest music out and we'll get started."

The fox was excited that he was about to hear their songs. He tried hard not to giggle out loud but his shoulders shook with excitement.

Trevor saw some of the tassels on the lamp-shade moving and cleverly guessed what was happening. He knew this was not a statue but the <u>real</u> naughty fox.

Then Trevor had one of his good ideas!

He said in a loud voice, "I'll just take off my left sock and put my foot in the basin of water as usual. I think I'll hang the sock on Declan's lovely new statue to keep it safe."

Trevor then went over and draped the stinky sock over the fox's piano-hands and returned to his place in the chorus.

The smell from Trevor's sock started to make the fox feel a bit sick but he managed to stay still.

The smell got worse and worse but he held on; desperate not to be discovered.

Mrs O'Hare tapped her baton on the music-stand but before they could all start singing there was a loud groan from the statue in the corner.

The smell of rotten fish and stinky cheese was too much to bear.

"AAAARRRGGGGHHH!

That's horrible!" shouted the fox.

He pulled the lamp-shade off his head, threw the sock on the floor and zoomed out of the door.

"Well, I never!" said Mrs O'Hare and the whole chorus burst out laughing.

Tali told them all the details of the competition; adding, "You'll be glad to hear it will take place here in Musselburgh."

Then he left them to their rehearsal. He wanted their contest songs to be a surprise too.

Chapter 7

The Dawn Chorus

When Tali went to visit *the Dawn Chorus* he had to walk through Princes Street Gardens. Every tree was full of birds singing … different songs.

What a racket they all made!

Tali spoke to a robin who was digging for worms to ask him what was going on.

"Well, the *Dawn Chorus* are having a rehearsal for the competition today," he replied.

"That's good," said Tali. "But, would it not be better for everyone to be quiet while they are singing?"

"No! We've seen Mr Fox and his Raptor-Rappers around and we don't want them to hear which songs we are practising. Bertie, up there, has asked all the birds in the gardens to make a noise to cover it up," he said, pointing up to the nest on the top of the Scott Monument.

Tali climbed up the 287 steps to the top of the stone tower and stepped into the large nest 200 feet above the ground. The nest was built with some of the entrance-feathers which birds had used to pay to compete in the Avian Games. It was called the Visitor Nest.

(Do remember why it was called this?)

(The nest was built to give birds who were visiting Edinburgh somewhere to sleep.)

Although it was a big nest, Tali wondered how 100 birds would fit inside especially if there were ostriches, emus or turkeys in the choir. He looked around and could see only one little bird there.

This was Bertie Blackbird, the director of *the Dawn Chorus*.

Bertie looked tiny standing all alone in the nest with his music-stand.

"Where are all the singers?" asked Tali.

"Over there," said Bertie, pointing across the road.

Tali looked across but he could not see any birds.

"Over where?" he asked Bertie.

"There! Look! On the ledges in front of the windows of the buildings."

Tali looked again and saw rows and rows of little birds lined up on the window-sills of the shops on the other side of Princes Street.

Thankfully, there were no turkeys, ostriches or emus. Tali did not like to think about the mess there would be if an ostrich did a huge, splashy poo whilst sitting on a high window-ledge.

"We decided to put a size limit on the members of the choir: no bigger than a pigeon. We also only wanted birds who can fly so they can join in the murmuration," explained Bertie.

"A fine selection of winged wonders," said Tali. "But why are you not down in the gardens?"

Bertie smiled and said, "I can hear the chorus from up here but they can't be heard from down below. Our friends are all singing loudly in the trees in the gardens. The noise they make means that our secret songs cannot be heard."

"Very clever," said Tali with a sly wink.

"Some nosey rascals (you know who) would love to hear what we are going to be singing in the competition," replied Bertie.

The birds on the window-sills were all watching carefully as Bertie waved his baton about majestically. His baton was really a lollipop stick but it seemed to work.

The Dawn Chorus were ready to sing!

Just then, a pair of beady eyes appeared over the edge of the nest.

It was the fox!

He had tied ten balloons to strings and was holding tightly onto them as he floated in the air in front of Bertie.

"Get out of it!" shouted the conductor-blackbird and hid his music sheets from the fox's gaze.

"Oh, please! Let me see what you are singing," said the fox. "I promise I'll not tell anyone."

"I've heard about your kind of promise. I don't believe you," shouted Bertie.

Suddenly, there was a flurry of wings as all the birds took off from their perches and attacked the intruder.

They pecked the fox's balloons with their beaks. Some of the balloons popped and the fox slowly started to drop to the ground. As more and more balloons were popped he dropped faster and faster, crying like a scaredy-fox.

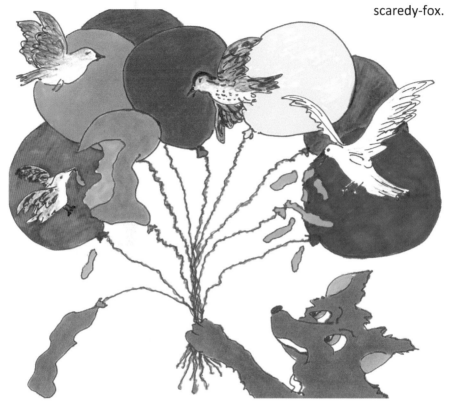

When the final balloon was burst, just before the fox hit the pavement, the birds caught the strings in their beaks and held him, floating in the air.

"Oh thanks," sighed the fox as the birds carried him upwards again.

But they did not stop at the top of the monument. They carried him all the way down to Silverknowes and dropped him into the sea.

SPLASH

The silly fox had to swim all the way back home to Musselburgh.

The birds returned to their perches and Bertie tapped his lollipop-baton on his music-stand.

He was about to put his music on the stand when Tali stopped him and pointed to the big hotel next to the monument.

"Look there!" he said to Bertie.

On the top floor window-sills sat the six raptor-rappers with binoculars.

They were trying to see Bertie's music sheets!

Tali ran down the 287 steps of the monument again and quickly nipped in the front door of the hotel.

He had noticed that some men were getting ready to wash the outside of the hotel's windows. The men were up on the roof with buckets of soapy water and long brushes.

Tali ran up to them and asked if he could borrow their buckets.

"Of course," they agreed. "But what do you want them for?"

"Watch this!" shouted Tali and grabbed the buckets of water.

He ran to the edge of the roof and poured the water over the side of the building, right onto the heads of the sneaky, cheating birds.

They were soaked!

The birds flew away back to the fox's house to tell him how they too had failed to discover any of *the Dawn Chorus*'s songs.

"Maybe we should give up," said an osprey.

"Never!" replied Mr Fox. "I come from a long line of naughty foxes. My father was a naughty fox and my grandfather was a naughty fox. We naughty foxes never give up … especially when there is £50 at stake."

Back in Edinburgh, all the birds cheered and clapped as Tali appeared from the hotel.

"Well done, Tali, our hero," they tweeted.

Tali had a long, interesting chat with *the Dawn Chorus* and explained that the contest was likely to take place in the theatre in Musselburgh.

"I hope that's not too far for you to travel," said Tali.

"Not at all. That's easy for us to get to; we can all just fly there," said Bertie Blackbird.

Tali wished them luck in the contest and wandered off to find Esmerelda.

Chapter 8

The Supercat Chorus

The final chorus that Tali had to visit was *the Supercat Chorus*. They rehearsed in Gerard's tool-shop which was downstairs from the flat where Misha Supercat lived.

(Do you remember the names of the people that Misha lived with?)

(Mr and Mrs Macdonald)

Now, in order to keep the Supercats' real identities secret, they all wore disguises. Some of the cats (like Misha) changed colour when they put on their Supercat costumes.

'Misha Cat'   'Misha Supercat'

Other cats (like Gerard) had masks but they <u>all</u> wore capes which made them able to fly.

It was only when the Supercats were wearing their capes that people and other animals could understand what they were saying. Otherwise, it just sounded like cat-speak:

(MWEH MWEH MWEH)

The singers could understand each other at all times so they could rehearse as ordinary cats but they had to wear their costumes to be able to perform for non-cats. So, being in a chorus was quite tricky for them and sometimes involved quick costume changes.

On the day they were expecting Tali to visit, all ten members were in their costumes. They were making a beautiful sound and Mr Macdonald could hear them from upstairs in his flat.

"I'm just popping downstairs to see who is doing all that lovely singing," he said to his wife.

When they heard his footsteps on the stairs, the Supercats quickly took off their costumes. Mr Macdonald must not find out that Misha and Gerard are superheroes! When he opened the door to the tool-shop all he saw was ten normal cats.

They were making a terrible racket!

(MWEH MWEH MWEH)

"Very strange," thought Mr Macdonald as he went back up the stairs, scratching his head.

Just then, Misha saw the roof of the library-van appear over the fence at the bottom of the garden.

"Quick everyone!" she shouted. "Tali is parking in the lane outside. Get into your Supercat costumes again."

Gerard was just fixing his mask when Tali came through the back door.

"Hello everyone. You all look very smart in your costumes," he said cheerfully. "I won't stay long. I just want to let you know that the contest will take place on Saturday in the theatre in Musselburgh. You should prepare a fast song and a slow song.

"On the day of the contest, the judges will let you know the order in which the competitors will perform.

"Now, do you have any questions for me?"

"Yes," asked Misha. "Who will be in the audience?"

"Well, the members of all the other choruses will be there. You can all sit in the audience when you are not performing. Everyone else will be able to buy tickets too," said Tali.

"That's good," said Misha. "I think Mr and Mrs Macdonald would like to come even though they won't recognise us in our costumes."

Tali could see that Gerard was getting fidgety and keen to start the rehearsal so he said 'goodbye' and opened the back door.

"Bye Tali. See you on Saturday," said Gerard as Tali headed for Esmerelda.

Misha was just about to tell the cats that they could take off their costumes when she noticed some beady eyes staring in at the window.

(Who do you think it was?)

It was some of the Rapper-Raptors who had come to spy on them.

Misha told the cats to keep their costumes on but to sing in cat-speak. She told them to sing: 'MWEH MWEH MWEH' instead of the proper words of the song.

This meant that the spies would not know what they were singing.

One vulture peered in the window through some binoculars (again) to try to see Gerard's music sheets but he could not read the name of the song on his music-stand.

This was because it was an Australian song. Gerard knew that Australia was on the other side of the world and so he thought that the music had to be played upside-down!

Silly Gerard … but lucky for the Supercats.

The cheating birds left empty-handed … again.

"We'll never win that £50," said Mr N Fox when he heard that they still did not know what anyone else was singing.

Chapter 9

Final Preparations

As the day of the competition approached, all the choruses used the final week to perfect their performances, both singing and 'dancing'. Remember, some choruses were doing gymnastics, flying or murmuration as part of their acts.

The Dancing Rabbit Chorus

Mrs O'Hare had chosen *'Halfway Down the Stairs'* as the slow song for her chorus. Trevor had been put in charge of the dancing (or 'choreography' as the Musical Director called it). All the rabbits started swaying slowly, in time with the tune.

As the song went on, they made a big pile of rabbits in the shape of a staircase.

At the end of the song, the smallest rabbit climbed up the 'rabbit-staircase' and sat on the middle step.

After a few attempts where the 'rabbit-hill' collapsed in a giggling mess, they became quite good at it.

Trevor had to be at the bottom of the pile so that his feet were not near any other rabbit's nose!

"Well done!" said Mrs O'Hare. "That's the slow song sounding quite good. Now let's concentrate on our other song; the fast one."

Their fast song was to be *'Let's Go Fly a Kite'*.

During this song, Declan had to spin his ten ears around like a helicopter so that he took off from the ground.

Trevor held on to a long piece of string tied to Declan's leg to pretend he was flying him as a kite.

Declan kept on banging his head on the ceiling and Mrs O'Hare thought that they should think of another idea.

Trevor said, "It will be fine on the day, Mrs No..... Mrs O'Hare. I've arranged something special with my cousin Martha Mouse. She always has a few tricks up her sleeve."

Trevor winked at Declan because they were the only two who knew that Martha was magical!

(I wonder what Trevor has planned, do you?)

The Rappers

The *Rappers* were not doing very well with their preparations.

They all sat around in the fox's sitting-room, wrapped in towels, drinking hot cups of tea.

The fox had just had to swim home after being dropped in the sea and the birds were soaked by the window-washing water which Tali had poured over them. They were all in bad moods.

"Does anyone know any songs?" asked a hawk.

"No," said the ospreys.

"Not a single one," said a vulture.

"Well, we all know *'Happy Birthday to You'*," said the fox. "How about singing that one? We could pretend it's my birthday!"

"Good idea!" they agreed.

"But, we need <u>two</u> songs: a slow one and a fast one," someone pointed out.

"Why don't we just sing *'Happy Birthday'* twice; once slowly, then again quickly," said a vulture, getting fed up with the whole idea of singing. "Or we could just steal the prize money!"

"Yeah, we're never going to <u>win</u> it anyway," said a hawk.

Just then the fox had a naughty idea.

"I think we should get revenge on Tali and the birds for soaking us," he said with a sneer. "We could hide up in the rafters just under the roof of the theatre with buckets of water and pour them down on the judges."

"That's what we'll do," they all chuckled. "The Revenge of the Rapper-Raptors in the Rafters."

The Dawn Chorus

Bertie Blackbird had chosen two songs which matched their chorus:

- Three Craws
    - A song about birds (crows)
- Here Comes the Sun
    - A song about the dawn

Bertie likes to watch quiz programmes on TV and thought it was 'Quite Interesting' when he found out that the Scottish word for 'Scotland' (Alba) is also the Italian word for 'dawn'. Bertie's granny is Italian and she had told him this when she found out the name of their chorus.

In Italian, *'The Dawn Chorus'* is 'Il Coro Dell'Alba'.

"So, here we are in Alba singing about the alba," he thought.

For the slow song, Bertie had thought about asking three real crows to join the chorus but then he heard them singing. They were awful!

Three blackbirds said they would play the part of the crows in the performance.

Bertie also wanted to make a huge murmuration sunrise for the fast song. He planned to have birds flying in all direction like the rays of the rising sun.

While they were practising this, one bird pointed out to him that the contest was not taking place outside.

It was being held in a theatre and there would not be much room for his huge ideas.

"Oh, yes. I didn't think of that," said Bertie. "Oh, well. We'll just have to fill the whole theatre, from the floor to the roof, with sunlight."

Bertie was beaming with pleasure and really enjoying being in charge of *the Dawn Chorus*!

His joy was infectious and all the birds were excited about the contest.

The Magical Musicians

As you know, Mary Mouse had chosen 'My Own Home' from the film called *'The Jungle Book'* for her choir's slow song.

Mary asked Martha to use her magic to make lots of trees and bushes to make it look like they were singing in a real jungle.

(Do you remember how Martha becomes magical?)

Martha twitched her nose until her whiskers turned gold and started to glow. As soon as she felt all tingly and magical, she said:

"Magic me a thick jungle!"

(Remember, Martha's spells all must begin with the letter 'M')

The library was suddenly filled with lots of tall trees and other plants.

Some of them had bright, red flowers while others had long, dangly tendrils hanging from high branches.

All the mice were amazed to see just how beautiful their scenery looked.

When they had finished their practice, Mary wondered how they were going to transport the 'jungle' to Scotland.

"Not a problem," said Martha as she shouted …

"Minimise the scenery!"

… and the jungle became so small she could put it into a little box and stick it in her pocket.

"I'll maximise it again when we're at the theatre," she told Mary.

Their fast song was *'The Wheels on the Bus'* and Martha was going to do some of her gymnastics along with it. She planned to do cartwheels to represent the wheels going round and round and star-jumps for the doors opening and shutting.

After the final practice, they were all pleased with their performance and looking forward to the contest.

The Supercat Chorus

For the slow, Australian song they were singing, Gerard thought that they should all be upside-down on the stage. Misha had to remind him that people in Australia were not really upside-down; they were just on the other side of the world.

The song was called *'Inanay Gupu Wanna'*, which traditional Australians used to sing to children to help them sleep. Misha suggested that they should gently sway from side to side while singing it.

Their swaying was so smooth and restful that Gerard almost fell asleep as he conducted the chorus.

By coincidence, the fast song the Supercats had chosen was also from the *'The Jungle Book'* film. It was called *'The Bare Necessities'*.

In the film, Baloo the Bear was floating down a river while singing this song.

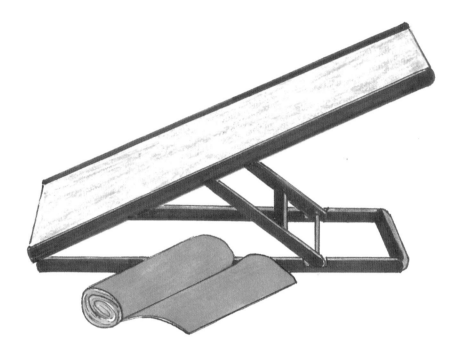

Gerard used his tools to build a little wooden ramp and lined it with blue paper to make it look like a river.

He then planned to have the other Supercats slide down the slope while they sang the song.

At the end of the practice, Gerard folded up the little ramp and rolled up the paper 'river', saying:

"Fellow Supercats, I believe we are ready for the Great Chorus Contest."

Then he added, "Bring it on!"

All the other Supercats whooped with excitement.

Chapter 10

Travel to Musselburgh – Part 1

At last, it was the day of the competition.

Tali and Esmerelda had parked beside the theatre over-night so that they would be there early.

The Local Musselburgh Choruses

The two local choruses were lucky because they did not need to travel far at all.

(Do you remember which two choruses are based in Musselburgh?)

(The Dancing Rabbit Chorus and of course the naughty Rappers)

All the other choruses were preparing to travel to Musselburgh.

The Magical Musicians

The London chorus had the furthest to travel but, fortunately, Martha (the Magical Mouse) knew a shortcut, called the 'Library Link'.

There was a door with this written on it in Camberwell Library, where they held their rehearsals. All Martha had to do was open the door while thinking hard about the place she wanted to travel to (Musselburgh).

All the mice from the chorus stood close together as Martha reached for the door-handle.

Just as Martha opened the door, Mary said:

"I remember when you used this magic link to visit your Granny Lucy in Corstorphine."

When the mice walked through the door into the other room, a sign on the wall said:

'Welcome to Corstorphine Library'.

Martha saw her Granny sitting at a desk, stamping books.

"Oh, hello Granny," she said. "I haven't come to visit you. I've just come here by mistake. My chatty friend, Mary, made me think of Corstorphine just as I opened the door."

"That's OK, Tootie-Pie," Granny replied. "I'll see you soon."

(Do you remember that Martha's Granny always calls her Tootie-Pie?)

They went back through the Library Link to Camberwell and Martha looked sternly at Mary, saying:

"No more talking as I open the door, please. I'm trying to concentrate on Musselburgh."

"Oops, sorry," said Mary as Martha reached for the handle again. "But, I'm so hungry. I really fancy a Paris Bun."

When the Library Link door opened for the second time, the sign on the wall said:

'Bienvenue à la Bibliothèque Centrale de Paris'

Martha did not speak much French but she knew that this meant 'Welcome to the Paris Central Library'.

"Goodness Gracious, Mary. You've done it again! You made me think of Paris buns just as I opened the magic door and here we are in the wrong library … again.

"We're supposed to be in Musselburgh, Scotland but here we are in Paris, France."

"Ooh La La," said Monica Mouse in a French accent. "I've never been to France before. Can we stay for a while? Please Martha!"

"That would be very nice, but remember we have a singing contest to enter. We must get to Musselburgh this morning," said Mary.

Martha pushed her friends back through the Library Link to London, saying, "Désolé Madame" to the very surprised French lady who had just seen five mice and a boy (with suitcases) appear through a door in her library.

Martha prepared herself to try again. "Right, Mary. Not a word," she said as she opened the door for the third time, thinking 'Musselburgh, Musselburgh, Musselburgh' to herself.

When the mice went through the Library Link door again, there was no sign on the wall to tell them where they were.

There was just a large sign saying LIBRARY on the wall along with posters for reading groups and other clubs.

"At least the signs are in English, not French, this time," said Melissa mouse with a giggle.

Martha walked up to the man at the desk and said, "Excuse me, Sir. Is this Musselburgh?"

"Yes, of course it's Musselburgh. Where else would it be?" he replied snippily.

"Well, frankly, it could be anywhere in the world when you're travelling with Mary 'Chatterbox' Mouse," she sighed.

Mary looked a bit miffed but she soon got over it and asked the man for directions to the hotel where they were to be staying.

The 'Magical Musicians' were excited; they were all in Musselburgh and the contest was that very afternoon! The mice friends all rushed along to their hotel to get unpacked and ready to sing (and dance).

"I hope you remembered to bring the little box with our 'minimised' scenery in it," Mary said to Martha.

"Don't worry, Mary, it's safely packed inside my suitcase," replied her friend.

Chapter 11

Travel to Musselburgh – Part 2

With three choruses now in Musselburgh, it was time for the two Edinburgh groups to set off.

The Dawn Chorus

Bertie had told all the birds to meet in Princes Street Gardens very early on the morning of the contest.

It was still dark when they met.

The plan was that the chorus would warm up their voices by singing as the sun rose.

They were a real 'dawn' chorus then.

Lots of people had heard about the contest and came to see them off. The people stood silently on all the streets around the gardens listening to the beautiful sound the birds made.

The mix of starlings, blackbirds, robins and wrens blending with sparrows, doves and pigeons made a marvellous harmony.

When the sun had fully risen and Edinburgh Castle was ablaze with sunshine, Bertie decided that *the Dawn Chorus* were ready for the competition. He raised his baton in the air and the whole chorus took to the skies and started the most wonderful murmuration.

The crowd gasped in awe as the swirling mass of individual birds formed more and more complex shapes.

Finally, there was a great roar of applause as the birds formed a treble-clef in the sky.

This is the musical symbol which shows the notes a piano player should play with his or her right hand.

It's a very difficult shape for the birds to make but they managed to maintain it as they soared higher and higher and then sped off towards Musselburgh by the sea.

The Supercat Chorus

The people of Corstorphine had also heard about the Great Chorus Contest and wanted to support their local group as they set off to compete.

Many of them lined the streets hoping to see the heroes in their costumes. People did not know where would be the best place to stand since no-one knew where the Supercats lived.

Luckily, Mr and Mrs Macdonald had decided to go out and join the crowds so they were not at home when the Supercats met in their flat. The chorus practised their songs a few times then Gerard declared that they were ready!

As you probably already know, Gerard had created a secret escape route which Misha uses when she leaves the Macdonalds' flat to go on missions. Misha pressed the special button which was hidden behind the curtain and the window flew open. The drain-pipe swung out over the garden and the trampoline slid into position over the fish-pond.

Everything was in position!

One by one the Supercats slid down the drain-pipe, bounced on the trampoline and flew into the air over the garden fence, shouting:

"Destination Musselburgh"

They formed a V-shape in the sky with Gerard at the front; their capes fluttering behind them.

Higher and higher over houses and woods the Supercats flew to the applause of the local people.

As they flew up over Corstorphine Hill, Misha spotted Mr and Mrs Macdonald sitting on a bench at the top. This seat gave them a great view over the whole city all the way to the sea in the distance.

The Macdonalds gasped with excitement when they saw the Supercats flying together overhead.

"If only Misha and Gerard had been up here with us today," said Mrs Macdonald. "They would have loved to see this."

She did not know that her favourite pet cats were right there, flying before her eyes.

Just then, Misha saw *the Dawn Chorus* ahead of them in the sky over Edinburgh.

She recognised their lovely musical treble-clef shape and whispered something to Gerard.

He nodded and quickly asked the Supercats to re-arrange their flying formation.

They formed the shape of a bass-clef with Gerard and Misha as the two dots in front.

This shape is the musical symbol which shows the notes a piano player should play with his or her <u>left</u> hand.

People on the ground cheered as they saw the two matching symbols and realised that the whole of Edinburgh was united in support of the city's two groups of musicians.

There was great excitement about the competition and lots of people from Princes Street and Corstorphine rushed to buy tickets for the Musselburgh theatre that afternoon.

Chapter 12

The Competition – First Half

All the choruses were now in Musselburgh, ready for the Great Chorus Contest.

People from all over Scotland were buying tickets and making their way into the theatre.

The competitors were warming up their voices by singing "La La La" very low and then very high; very quietly and then very loudly.

(Can you do that?)

The naughty *Rappers* filled their buckets with water from a tap in the theatre's kitchen and sneaked them up into the rafters above the stage.

Nobody noticed them because they were all too busy preparing for the contest.

As the theatre was filling up, Martha decided that it was time to return the jungle scenery to its normal size. All she had to do was cancel the spell that she had used to make it small.

(Do you remember how Martha cancels one of her spells?)

(Yes, she says the spell backwards.)

She has used a 'Minimise the Scenery' spell to make it fit into the box, so she needed to say 'Scenery the Minimise' to cancel the spell.

Martha took the little box out of her pocket and placed it on the stage.

Making sure everyone was well out of the way (and that no-one could see her) she made herself magical and shouted:

"Scenery the Minimise!"

In an instant, the jungle returned to its normal size and filled the stage with trees and flowers.

Gerard immediately recognised the scenery from *'The Jungle Book'* and asked if the Supercats could borrow it for their performance since they were singing a song from that film too.

"Of course you can," said Mary.

Gerard quickly added his blue, paper river to the jungle scene on the stage and Martha said that she thought it looked splendid beside her plants.

When the audience had taken their seats in the theatre along with the members of each chorus, Tali announced the scoring system for the contest.

There would be 20 points available for each chorus; 10 for singing and 10 for presentation.

He also announced that he would <u>not</u> be judging the competition after all.

"I feel that I have so many friends in each of the choruses that it would not be right for me to choose the winner," he said. "So, I have asked two of the finest singers in Scotland to be judges."

"Please welcome ... Anne Hayes and Rosalind Johnson."

There was great applause as the two ladies took their seats beside Tali at the front of the stage.

The *Rappers* could see down from the rafters. They were directly above Tali and the judges!

Tali then announced that the order of the choruses' performances in the contest would be:

1. *The Magical Musicians*
2. *The Supercat Chorus*
3. *The Dancing Rabbit Chorus*
4. *The Dawn Chorus*
5. *The Rappers*

"Can I ask the first chorus to come up and sing their two songs," he said and Mary's group of friends stood up and made their way onto the stage.

Then Tali shouted:

"Let the Great Chorus Contest begin!"

Mary raised her spoon-baton and the mice started singing *'My Own Home'*. Martha decided to add some more colour to the jungle. She used one of her special 'Miggly' spells which turn her into other animals.

(Remember… it's 'Miggly Mox' for a fox; 'Miggly Mebra' for a zebra)

"Miggly Marrot!"

… she shouted and turned herself into a beautiful parrot.

Suddenly, Peter noticed that a river had been added to their jungle scenery. He got a bit excited and decided to play the part of the boy 'Mowgli' from the film. In the story, Mowgli fell out of a tree into the river.

Peter climbed up the scenery and jumped into Gerard's paper river. Sadly, he was too heavy and his feet tore a big hole in it.

The audience thought it was very funny but Mary was not pleased!

Gerard, watching from the audience, was not pleased either. He planned to use that river for Baloo the Bear singing *'The Bare Necessities'* and now the paper was ripped to pieces.

While Mary was pulling Peter out of the 'river', Martha Parrot flew out over the audience to distract their attention from what was happening on the stage.

She flew up high and saw the Raptors in the rafters with their buckets of water; right above Tali and the judges. Martha knew they were plotting something and wanted to find out what it was.

She could see that Mary was getting ready for their next song so she quickly changed back into a mouse and returned to the stage.

When their second song started, Martha did her gymnastic cartwheels in front of the chorus. She got faster and faster and finally rolled right behind the scenery at the side of the stage. She climbed up the jungle trees and into the rafters of the theatre roof just as the fox and his chums were starting to pour the water from their buckets.

She made herself magical and shouted:

"Move the Waterfall"

The falling water from the seven buckets joined together in mid-air. The single stream fell with a splash onto the top of Gerard's wooden ramp and poured down the slope.

What was left of the ripped, blue paper dissolved in the water and made a beautiful, real river. Magically, when the water reached the bottom of the ramp, it just went back up and flowed down again.

Up in the rafters, the raptors stared at Martha, afraid of what she might do next.

Martha was very angry and shouted:

"Minimise the Rappers"

Mr Fox and his six feathered friends were reduced to the size of ants.

Martha picked them up and put them in her little scenery box.

She popped them in her pocket and star-jumped back onto the stage just as *'The Wheels on the Bus'* was finishing.

The audience were amazed and clapped loudly as Mary curtseyed then led her chorus off the stage.

"What's going on?" she whispered to Martha as they returned to their seats.

"I'll tell you later, Mary," replied Martha. "I need to do some more magic soon."

Tali and the judges had no idea how close they had come to being soaked.

When Gerard's chorus went up onto the stage, they were amazed to see real water pouring down the ramp he had made. So was Gerard!

"How did he do that?" they asked Misha.

"I'm not sure. But, you can never be sure with Gerard's inventions," she replied proudly. Gerard was happy to take the credit for making a real flowing river.

The *Supercats* sang their swaying, Australian lullaby beautifully and the sound of trickling water in the background made it even more soothing. Lots of people started to feel sleepy while listening to it.

Mr Macdonald was fast asleep and snoring loudly in the audience by the end of the song.

His embarrassed wife had to elbow him in the ribs and shout loudly at him:

"Wake up, you silly old man"

He woke up with a fright and wondered where he was.

When the Supercats started to sing 'Bare Necessities', they were not sure if they were supposed to slide down the <u>real</u> river or not; remember, it had been made of paper, not water, during their practice sessions.

Most of them decided that they would follow whatever Misha did.

She stood at the top of the slope and gentle lowered herself into the flowing water. Then, she slid down on her bottom, singing at the top of her voice.

The other Supercats followed and it was great fun.

Then, they all went back to the top of the ramp and slid down on their backs, just like Baloo had done in the film.

The audience loved it and cheered loudly when the song ended.

So far, the competition was a great success. Two choruses had performed and both had done very well.

Next, Tali announced that there would be a short interval and that people could buy drinks and ice-creams if they wished.

Chapter 13

The Competition – Second Half

After the interval, Tali asked everyone to take their seats as the contest was about to re-start. An excited hush fell over the crowd.

The Dancing Rabbit Chorus

As Mrs O'Hare led her chorus onto the stage, Tali announced, "Here we have a local Musselburgh chorus, *the Dancing Rabbit Chorus*. They are led by Mrs Ida ….

("I didn't know her first name was 'Ida'," thought Trevor.)

… Lott

("I didn't know she <u>had</u> a second name," thought Declan.)

… O'Hare.

Trevor and Declan nearly burst out laughing when they hear Mrs O'Hare's full name but one stern stare from her was enough to make them think again.

Their first song (the slow one) went very well. They succeeded in building the staircase with no trouble and the little rabbit managed to sit on the step half-way down. To be extra sure that there was no smell, Trevor stuck his left foot into the bottom of the 'jungle river' and kept it there throughout the whole song.

During 'Let's Go Fly a Kite', the audience gasped with excitement when Declan started rising in the air. Mrs O'Hare was starting to get concerned that Declan would hit the roof so she glanced over at Trevor.

He had told her not to worry; that his cousin had a 'trick' up her sleeve.

Trevor just smiled and nodded his head at Martha in the audience. She twitched her whiskers and whispered:

"Move the Roof"

Slowly, the roof of the theatre split in two and started to slide apart. Declan flew up through the roof and out of the theatre into the sky over Musselburgh. Higher and higher he flew until Trevor had no more string left.   Then Trevor started to rise up in the air too.

The other rabbits had to grab his feet (well, his right foot) and pull him back down.

As the song ended, Declan slowly came back through the roof and landed on the stage. The audience went wild and even the judges were on their feet, clapping.

Bertie Blackbird called his chorus onto the stage.

While the large flock of birds arranged themselves in the jungle trees (and one or two took a last-minute drink from the river), he turned to the audience and said:

"I don't know who arranged for the roof to be opened but please don't shut it yet. Can you leave it just like that for our performance? Thank you."

Martha secretly smiled to herself and was happy to help Bertie.

When the birds sang *'Three Craws',* lots of people in the audience joined in the singing because they all knew the words.

"I remember my Grampa singing this to me when I was a boy," sighed Mr Macdonald, wistfully.

"You silly old sausage," said his wife, but she had a tear in her eye too.

The Dawn Chorus then sang *'Here Comes the Sun'*.

While they were singing, every bird secretly put a little finger-torch on the tip of each wing. When they reached the final verse, they switched the torches on and flew out over the audience in a colourful murmuration.

The theatre was ablaze with light, just like a real sunrise.

They audience loved the spectacle!

They jumped to their feet and shouted for the chorus to sing it again.

"Encore, Encore!"

Bertie was happy to repeat the song.

He tapped his lollipop-stick-baton on his music stand and there was silence in the theatre. Well, almost silence: the only sound was the quiet ticking of the clock on the wall.

Bertie raised his hands and *the Dawn Chorus* began to sing again.

This time, the glorious sunrise murmuration rose up and right out through the open roof of the theatre.

The birds flew all over the town, the Links and the beach.

People in every part of Musselburgh gasped and cheered when they saw the beautiful display.

When the birds finally flew back in through the roof and returned to the stage, the audience were still standing and clapping.

Bertie took a bow and said, with tears in his eyes:

"Grazie dal coro dell'alba … Thank you from *the Dawn Chorus*."

It was now time for the final performance of the contest and Tali announced:

"Please welcome to the stage ... *'The Rappers'*."

Nothing happened so he repeated it louder:

"Please welcome to the stage ... *'The Rappers'*."

Still, nobody appeared.

Tali finally noticed a little box sitting in the middle of the stage.

Martha had put it there while everyone was watching Bertie Blackbird make a long, rambling speech about how much he loved his Granny Blackbird (or 'Nonna Merla' as he called her).

Tali walked over and opened the box. Seven little 'ants' climbed out and sat on Tali's upturned paw.

They started to sing but their little, tiny voices could not be heard by anyone.

Tali signalled for the audience to be quiet and then they could hear the very tiny voices singing *'Happy Birthday to You'* extremely quietly and slowly.

The singing was so quiet that someone had to go and put a thick blanket over the clock on the wall of the theatre to stop it ticking.

Mrs Macdonald was very pleased that her husband had stopped snoring or else no-one would have heard the song. She gave him another nudge to make sure he was awake and one of her best stares as a warning to behave himself.

"But, but, I haven't done anything wrong," he muttered quietly to himself.

When the mini-Rappers had finished singing, Martha cancelled her spell by saying:

"Rappers the Minimise"

The *Rappers* instantly returned to their normal size.

All the raptor birds flew up into the jungle trees and looked very dizzy and confused about what had happened to them. They did <u>not</u> look very happy and quickly decided that they would not be singing anymore.

Mr Fox could not fly so he just stayed where he was.

Poor Tali had a full-size Fox sitting on his paw!

Being back to his normal size, the fox was very, very heavy.

Tali could not hold the fox up any longer and had to drop him onto the stage.

Tali washed his hands in the jungle-river and returned to his seat beside the judges.

The naughty Mr Fox looked very surprised and felt a bit nervous as he stood alone on the stage.

Suddenly, he noticed everyone in the audience staring at him expectantly. He waved to the raptors to come and join him but they just shook their heads and stayed in the jungle-trees.

Finally, Mr Fox cleared his throat and started singing on his own.

He remembered what the *Rappers* had decided for their second song so he sang *'Happy Birthday to You'* again; loudly and quickly.

As he sang, he staggered about the stage because he was still a bit dizzy from being 'minimized' to the size of an ant.

Suddenly, he tripped over the bottom of Gerard's blue river and fell face-first into the water.

He was soaked ... again!

The audience (and the raptors in the jungle trees) roared with laughter to see the fox staggering about the stage, dripping wet and trying to sing with his mouth full of water.

Their laughter woke up Mr Macdonald who had fallen asleep again. When he heard the song, he said, "It's not <u>my</u> birthday, is it?"

"Oh be quiet, you silly man," said his wife, yet again.

Poor old Mr Macdonald.

Chapter 14

The Results

When Mr Fox had finished his solo performance, he bowed to the audience, ran off the stage and grabbed a towel to dry himself. The raptors flew down from the trees and joined him in the audience.

People clapped politely and then Tali announced that the judges were about to decide the results of the contest.

Anne and Rosalind had a long chat and then produced a sheet of paper with the scores:

Chorus Name	Singing	Presentation	Total
The Magical Musicians	7	7	14
The Supercat Chorus	8	6	14
The Dancing Rabbit Chorus	5	9	14
The Dawn Chorus	6	8	14
The Rappers	2	6	8

Tali invited the judges to make a few comments.

Rosalind Johnston said that <u>most</u> of the singing was good and <u>most</u> of the presentations were excellent.

"The last chorus were given only two points for singing because we could not really hear their first song and we could not see them at all. We had no idea where they were hiding. Their second song was sung too quickly and by a solo fox, not a group," she added.

Anne Hayes then said, "Yes, we gave the '*Rappers*' six out of ten for presentation because we had no idea where they suddenly appeared from. Very impressive, almost like magic. All the other choruses got fourteen points each. It's a draw! This has been more a celebration of music than a competition."

Everyone in the audience clapped politely because they all agreed with these reviews of the performances.

"Now it's time for the prize," said Tali.

"I wonder if they'll split the prize four ways since there were four winners," thought the fox to himself.

Then he shouted out, "Why don't you just give the money to the group that came last? We deserve it the most, don't you think?"

"Money?" asked Tali. "What Money?"

"The £50 prize, of course," said the greedy fox, licking his lips.

"The prize is 50 pounds of potatoes, look!" said Tali.

APPLY BY NEXTFRIDAY To:
MR. TALI BOOKHOUND,
ESMERELDA,
TRAVELLING AROUND
SCOTLAND

APPLICATION FORMS IN
THE BAG BELOW

PRIZE 50 POUNDS OF POTATOES

Tali held up the poster which had been stuck to the side of Esmerelda.

The Rappers then realised that a corner of the paper had been curled up in front of the words '<u>of potatoes</u>' when they had seen it.

"The prize has been kindly donated by Guy the Gardener. For those of you who don't know Guy, he is a young man who once borrowed a book from my library because he wanted to learn how to grow vegetables. Now he grows lots of different types," added Tali. "Here he is!"

Guy stepped up onto the stage beside Tali and said he was delighted to be involved with such a great event and thanked Tali for organising it.

He also presented each of the judges with a large bunch of flowers and said:

"These flowers are from my garden. I'm glad it's not <u>flour</u> this time."

Mr Fox's face became even redder than it usually is because it was he who had mistakenly thrown flour instead of flowers onto the stage at the end of Tali's play.

Guy announced, "The potatoes are outside the theatre on the grassy area called 'the Links' beside the beach. The have all been baked and are ready to eat."

"Everyone is welcome to come and have a picnic with us," added Tali.

Everyone lined up at Esmerelda's door as Tali and Guy served up the tasty potatoes.

Most of the friends sat on the grass in groups and chatted about their favourite song in the contest.

(Can you recognise everyone in the picture?)

As well as the baked 'prize' potatoes, Guy had provided sunflower seeds for the birds to eat, even though the larger birds had been naughty and did not really deserve them. The raptors said they were sorry for trying to soak the judges and then they pecked up all the seeds.

The Macdonalds had brought a large box of fish-fingers for the picnic. Misha and Gerard were still in their Supercat disguises so Mrs Macdonald did not recognise them.

"I have a cat at home, you know," she told them. "Her name is Misha and fish-fingers are her favourite food. I wish she could have been here today."

Gerard started to giggle but Misha just purred and said, "MWEH-MWEH."

When no-one was looking, Martha magicked up a huge chocolate cake which she shared with the other choruses. But only after Mary Mouse had scoffed three large slices of it.

When it was time to leave, *the Magical Musicians* thanked Tali and the judges for making the *'Great Chorus Contest'* especially great and headed for Musselburgh library.

Mary kept talking about how much she enjoyed meeting Trevor and Declan again. She talked so much that Martha had to tell her to be quiet while she got ready to open the door to the magic Library Link.

Martha still found it hard to concentrate on her spell and so there were quite a few visits to other libraries before they found themselves back home in Camberwell.

Trevor and Declan were teasing Mrs O'Hare about her name. They stood next to the table while she was eating her potato and spoke very loudly to each other.

"That was a great picnic," said Trevor. "I had a lot of beans."

"Yes," replied Declan. "Ida Lott O'Beans, too."

Mrs Ida Lott O'Hare just ignored them and carried on chatting to Tali and the judges, Anne and Rosalind.

When everyone had finished their picnic, there was a lot of rubbish lying on the grass on the links.

"Oh look," said Tali. "There are hundreds of food wrappers."

"It's just as well we have our own team of Rappers to pick them all up."

He handed Mr Fox and his naughty friends long, pointy sticks and made them clear up all the mess.

THE END

More Bedtime Stories

The Rabbit with Three Ears

The Rabbit with Three Ears gets up to tricks with other rabbits, pigeons, a seagull, a fox, a dog, a mole and a cat.

Martha, the Magical Mouse

Martha the Mouse discovers that she can do magical things (sometimes).

She and her musical friend, Mary, have lots of adventures in London and elsewhere.

She visits her cousin Trevor, the Rabbit with Three Ears, during the Edinburgh Festival and they all take a camping trip to the island of Arran.

Misha Supercat

Misha looks like an ordinary pet cat but she is really a superhero.

She and her side-kick Gerard rescue and advise people in need all over Edinburgh.

Gerard is a really clumsy cat but he tries to copy Misha as they perform their various missions.

He dreams of becoming a real superhero too.

Tali Bookhound

Tali runs a mobile library from an old camper-van called 'Esmeralda' which he drives from town to town.

When people come to choose books, he helps them to find the right one.

The books are magic and often take Tali and his friends off on exciting adventures.

The Avian Games

Birds decide to hold a series of competitions like the Olympic Games.

Owls, pelicans, emus, penguins, robins, flamingos, geese and hummingbirds all have different talents when it comes to sports.

Other birds, like vultures, hawks and ospreys are only good at one thing ..... cheating!

They try to spoil the Avian Games for everyone else.

But, will they succeed?

Printed in Great Britain
by Amazon

60651399R00048